D0511929

THIS **Picture Knight** BOOK
BELONGS TO

....

Just like Jasper!

Nick Butterworth and Mick Inkpen

Picture Knight

HODDER AND STOUGHTON

Jasper is going to the toyshop with his birthday money.

What will
he buy?

Will he choose a ball?

Or perhaps a
clockwork mouse?

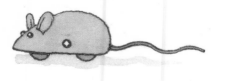

A noisy drum?

Or some bubbles?

Would he like a car?

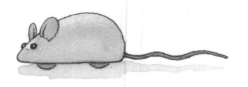

Or maybe a doll?

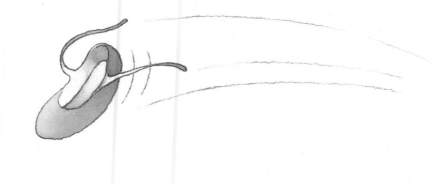

Or a robot?

Will he choose a Jack-in-a-box?

No. Jasper doesn't want any of these.

What has he chosen?

It's a little cat.
Just like Jasper!

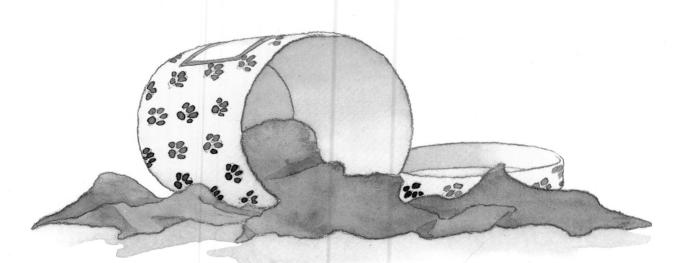

British Library Cataloguing in Publication Data

Butterworth, Nick
Just like Jasper!
I. Title   II. Inkpen, Mick
823'.914[J]

ISBN 0-340-52582-7

First published 1989 by Hodder and Stoughton Children's Books
Picture Knight edition first published 1990
12 11 10 9 8 7 6 5

Published by Hodder and Stoughton Children's Books,
a division of Hodder and Stoughton Ltd,
Mill Road, Dunton Green, Sevenoaks, Kent TN13 2YA

Printed in Italy by L.E.G.O., Vicenza

Other Picture Knight titles by Nick Butterworth and Mick Inkpen:

The Nativity Play
Nice and Nasty
Sports Day
The School Trip
Jasper's Beanstalk

and by Mick Inkpen:

One Bear at Bedtime
The Blue Balloon
Threadbear
Kipper
Kipper's Toybox